Ideal for animal lovers

Full of Christmassy magic

Beautiful illustrations that will really get you in the festive spirit

Lucy helps a lost otter cub

Make a wish

D0956198

Here's a taste of the magic to come . . .

Lucy ran as fast as she could back to her house and up the stairs to her bedroom. There, beside her bed, was her snow globe. It was a beautiful glass

globe with a forest and a little house inside, and when she shook it snow fell—but Lucy knew that sometimes it had a way of making special things happen, and she hoped so much that it could help her now.

"I know there's something magic about you at Christmas," said Lucy, sitting on the bed and picking it up. "And it's Christmas time now and I really need you to do magic. PLEASE magic snow globe—help that poor little otter get better." She closed her eyes as she made her wish and shook the globe.

Read on to find out if Lucy gets her wish . . .

To Oliver, Thea, Adam, and Esme
And to Theo and Saffy Haynes

ISBN 978-1-338-61904-1

12 11 10 9 8 7 6 5 4 3 2 1   19 20 21 22 23 24

Printed in the U.S.A.   40

First Scholastic printing, November 2019

LUCY'S WINTER RESCUE

Anne Booth

SCHOLASTIC INC.

Chapter One

It was the week before Christmas, and Lucy and her friend Sita had gone to play at their friend Rosie's house for the afternoon.

It was always fun at Rosie's. She lived in a house by the river with her mom, and her stepdad, Peter. Peter and her mom had a little baby, so Rosie had a little sister, Leah. Everybody loved Leah. She was only two and a half and loved dressing up and playing with Rosie and her friends. Today Leah wanted to be Father Christmas's baby reindeer and

live under the table, so the girls took it in turns to pretend to feed her and give her lots of special hugs. She was so sweet.

"Me baby rabbit now!" said Leah, coming out from under the table, jumping around the room.

"Leah would love my gran's Wildlife Rescue Center!" laughed Lucy. "We have a wild rabbit with a sore ear there now."

"She'd love your uniform and the badges your gran makes for it too!" laughed Rosie. "What animal badges have you got now?"

"Well, I've got badges for helping a magpie with a broken wing, and a newt, and we're looking after lots of tiny hedgehogs, so Gran is making me a hedgehog badge. I've got my rabbit badge already because of the little baby rabbit I rescued last Christmas."

"That was when I had just arrived from Australia," said Sita. "I remember that little rabbit!"

"Me RABBIT!" shouted Leah.

"Why don't you be a sleeping bunny?" said Rosie, and she played a song on the piano about little bunnies being asleep.

"Everybody sleeping bunnies!" said Leah, and she made Lucy and Sita lie down beside her and pretend to be asleep. Leah looked very sweet and Lucy made Sita laugh by pretending to snore.

Then, when Rosie sang the waking up words "Hop little bunny, hop, hop, hop!", Lucy and Sita had to jump up and down with Leah, who thought it was the best fun ever and kept hopping and hopping and laughing and laughing so that they all laughed too.

"Again! Again!" said Leah, but just at that moment, Rosie's mom came in.

"Thanks so much for playing with Leah, girls, but I think she might need a little nap now."

"NO!" shouted Leah. "Me bunny. Me HOP. Me not go bed." Her face turned very red and she started to cry.

"Girls—I don't think she will settle if

she thinks you are in the house. Do you think you could go and find some holly and ivy for me? I saw quite a lot growing next to the river the other day. I thought we might use it to help decorate the church for Christmas, and you can bring back some for your homes if you like. I'll give you some scissors and some thick gloves and this bag to put them in. Now girls, be careful not to get too near the river—it's gotten a lot higher lately. I think it's all the rain we've been having. I know you'll be sensible."

The girls put on their warm coats and hats and scarves and went down Rosie's garden to her back gate and out onto

the wide path by the river. They could
still hear little Leah's wailing: "No! No
sleep! Want GIRLS! Want DOGGY!"

"What does she mean?" said Sita.
"You don't have a dog."

"She keeps saying there's a dog in the garden," said Rosie. "But we've never seen one."

"Poor Leah—she sounds so upset," said Lucy.

"She'll be all right after her nap," said Rosie, closing the gate behind her. "She just got a bit too excited doing that song."

"You're such a good singer," said Sita.

"Um," said Rosie, and made a face.

"What's the matter?" said Lucy.

"It's just that Mom and I are in the church choir, and we're going to sing carols at Forest Lodge—the old people's home my grandad's in. We're going to sing to them on Christmas Eve—and they want me to sing a solo."

"That's great!" said Sita.

"You're so good at music! You'll be brilliant!" said Lucy.

Rosie bit her lip. "I don't know—I'm just really worried. What if it all goes wrong and I let everyone down? Grandad has been telling everyone in the home about my singing. Mom and Peter say I will be fine, and even Dad is coming to see me. But what if I forget the words or sing out of tune? I'm so scared I keep having bad dreams and waking up and worrying about it."

Just then Lucy heard a strange little cry coming from the riverbank—a faint, very high-pitched call, a bit like a cross between a whistle and a whimper.

"Did you hear that?" she said. A red-breasted robin hopped onto a bush nearby and started singing.

"That's a robin," said Sita. "That's so Christmassy!"

"No, I meant the first noise. Listen." The girls stopped. The faint high noise came again, along with some tiny splashes.

"It's coming from those reeds on the riverbank near us," said Lucy.

"Is it a water vole?" said Rosie. "I remember you told us Ratty in *The Wind in the Willows* was one."

"I don't think it's a water vole," said Lucy, turning in the direction of the cries and carefully making her way down the riverbank. "I'd love to see one but Gran and I have looked and there are no burrows or droppings or tracks along this bit of the river. There are no feeding stations either, where they leave piles of stems of grass. But I think I may have an idea what it is. I think this animal is in *The Wind in the Willows* too. I just hope it isn't in trouble."

"Be very careful," said Rosie. "Mom told us to stay away from the river."

Lucy reached the riverbank, and peered into the reeds right at the edge. At first she could only see some trash—a potato chip bag and a beer can—but then…

"Oh no!" said Lucy. "This is awful. Can you pass me the gloves and the scissors, Rosie?"

Rosie and Sita carefully made their way down the bank to where Lucy was, and looked over her shoulder into the reeds. There, struggling to keep its head above the water, and trapped in the reeds, with some plastic trash around its neck, was a small furry animal.

"I was right—it's a baby otter!" said Lucy. "I've never seen one so small. Gran told me they stay in their holt—that's their home—for about three months, so this one shouldn't be out alone at all. We've got to get it out of those reeds and keep it warm—look how it's shivering."

"What should we do?" said Sita.

"I'm going to put on the thick gloves," Lucy replied. "It looks too tiny and weak to bite me but I'm not taking any chances: I know otter teeth are really sharp. Gran told me about a friend of hers who had to go to the hospital when a grown-up otter bit her. Then I'm going to lift it out and hold it and you can cut the plastic off from around its neck."

Lucy put on the gloves and lifted

the baby otter out. Lucy had learned from
her gran how to hold animals gently but
firmly so they couldn't bite. Sita carefully
cut the plastic off its neck. It was too weak

to struggle much and its poor little neck looked sore. Its fur was dark and sodden, and it was shivering.

"Here," said Rosie, taking off her hat and scarf. "Let's wrap it up and bring it home quickly. You can call your gran from my house, Lucy."

"It's very ill," said Lucy, as they rushed back up the path. "It might not even know how to swim yet—they don't learn until they are about ten weeks old and they are blind until they are four or five weeks old. Gran was teaching me about them last night. I didn't think I'd see one so soon. I wonder how old this one is."

Back at Rosie's house, Lucy called

Gran and told her what they had found. Gran headed over right away. Rosie found a cardboard box and a towel. They unwrapped the baby otter from Rosie's hat and scarf and tried to blot the excess water from its dark fur. It kept its eyes closed and didn't struggle.

"I'm so sorry girls, but it's very ill," said Gran. "It is so small—about nine weeks old—that I think the river water must have risen and washed this little cub out of its holt and downstream, and into the reeds and the trash. It shouldn't be outside yet. And it is so cold and that awful plastic has rubbed against its poor little neck and made it sore. I'll bring it back to the Center now and I'll phone the vet. I think it will need an antibiotic injection to help it fight any infection it may have."

Rosie and Sita looked upset. "We're going to save it!" said Lucy confidently. "I know we can. I'll go back with Gran now but I'll tell you all about it tomorrow—I promise."

Lucy picked up the box and whispered, so that only the otter could hear. "Don't worry—I have a magic snow globe and as soon as I get home I am going to wish on it for you. You'll be better for Christmas—I know you will!"

Chapter Two

Gran and Lucy went back to Gran's house, and went through to the Wildlife Rescue Center at the back. Even though it was a working sanctuary it still looked Christmassy—Lucy had made and hung up some red and silver and green and gold paper chains along the walls, and Gran had put up a Christmas tree in the corner with little animal treats wrapped up in Christmas paper hanging from the branches.

The rabbit with a sore ear hopped to the side of its cage and wiggled its nose as they came in; a sleeping owl that had hurt its leg opened its eyes and closed them again; and the five little hedgehogs snuffled around in their special cages.

"Take that warm towel from the radiator, Lucy," said Gran, "and put it on the bottom of this heated cage. Check the cage temperature is about 86°F. We don't want to overheat him but he needs to get warm. He won't feed if he is cold."

Then Gran carefully lifted the sick little otter and placed him into the cage.

"Will he be OK, Gran?" Lucy said. She didn't feel so confident anymore. He looked so sick and his breathing wasn't very good. Lucy felt her eyes fill with tears. It was so sad to see him looking so ill.

"I don't know, Lucy, love, but I hope so," said Gran. "I'll call the vet. He's in the warm and dry now. There is not much we can do now for him until he warms up a bit."

I know something I can do, thought Lucy suddenly. "I'll be back in five minutes, Gran," she said, and ran out of the house.

Lucy ran as fast as she could back to her house and up the stairs to her bedroom. There, beside her bed, was her snow globe. It was a beautiful glass globe with a forest and a little house inside,

and when she shook it snow fell—but Lucy knew that sometimes it had a way of making special things happen, and she hoped so much that it could help her now.

"I know there's something magic about you at Christmas," said Lucy, sitting on the bed and picking it up. "And it's Christmas time now and I really need you to do magic. PLEASE magic snow globe—help that poor little otter get better." She closed her eyes as she made her wish and shook the globe. She had shaken it many times during the year and nothing magic had happened—but now as she shook it she felt her hands tingling as it grew warm. It was working! She opened her eyes and she saw the snow falling inside the globe start to glow and whirl and sparkle and change from white to silver, green, and red and all the different colors of the rainbow.

Suddenly the glittering snow cleared completely and even the house and the wood disappeared. Instead, for a moment she was sure she saw in the globe a little red car driving down a road and stopping outside her gran's door. She blinked, and the car and Gran's house had gone. All she could see was white snow falling on a little house in a wood again. It was almost as if she had imagined it. But her hands still tingled and inside she suddenly felt extremely happy, as if someone had told her a most wonderful secret . . . she wasn't sure what it was but she knew it was good.

She quickly pulled on her Wildlife Rescue Center sweatshirt, put the globe in her coat pocket, and rushed back to Gran's. As she got there Gran was just waving off a little red car. It was the same car Lucy had seen in her snow globe!

"You'll never guess what happened, Lucy!" said Gran, smiling. "Just after you left, before I even got through to the vet's office, the vet stopped by with a Christmas card. She took a look at the otter and she gave him an injection of antibiotics. She said that you found him just in time, as he could have given up struggling and drowned, and that the antibiotics will help him. I can't help feeling he looks better already!"

The snow globe granted my wish, thought Lucy excitedly as she watched the baby otter. He seemed to like it in the warm, stretching his little legs out. He gave a

little wriggle. Lucy watched and saw his fur begin to dry out, changing color from dark to light brown, spiking a little like a hedgehog.

"He's so sweet!" said Lucy, peering in.

"He is—but if we can get him to pull through he needs rehoming somewhere else quickly," said Gran. "If we raise him on his own he will be too used to humans and follow us about."

"But wouldn't it be lovely if we could have a pet otter?" said Lucy. "Imagine him following me to school—all the children would want one!"

"Not when he got older, Lucy," said Gran. "Their teeth are very sharp and their jaws are very powerful. They can bite and badly hurt people even without meaning to. They are shy, mysterious, beautiful animals. They need other otters and wild spaces and water."

Lucy looked in at the little otter. "Do you think we can get him back home before Christmas?"

"I'm not sure we'll be able to find his home, Lucy. We don't know where he has come from. The flooded river may have swept him down into the village from the wilder countryside. Even if we found his holt nearer the village then we couldn't be sure it was his, and we can't approach it and disturb any other otters in it. We need to find an otter sanctuary as soon as possible. I'll give my old friend, Tom, a call this afternoon—we used to work together in his otter sanctuary. I do hope he'll be able to help."

"While the little otter is at the Center could I help look after him as well as the tiny hedgehogs?"

"Of course! And then I will give you an otter badge to go with the hedgehog badge and the others. You're so good at looking after animals, Lucy. Look at how much weight the little hedgehogs have put on since you started helping! We'll be able to release them into safe gardens in the spring and they will go back to eating the slugs and helping the lucky gardeners. Then next winter they will be fat enough to hibernate. They will sleep through until the following spring thanks to all your hard work."

Lucy beamed. She loved learning about wildlife from Gran. Normally she wore her special uniform when she came to clean out the cages or feed the animals. In the winter they had lots of baby or underweight hedgehogs who were too small to hibernate. They needed feeding and keeping warm, and each time they put a hedgehog on the scales it was Lucy's job to carefully write down in a book how much it weighed. It was lovely to feel and see them getting heavier.

The otter wriggled and made a tiny weak chittering noise.

"Can I feed it?" said Lucy. "What will it eat, Gran?"

"It's still very tiny, so we will give it a syringe of glucose and water first, and then the special puppy-rearing milk will be fine. We can mix it with a little raw, flaked fish and feed it from a spoon— and we will have to do it every hour at first. It will be a lot of work."

"I'll help!" said Lucy eagerly.

Gran held the otter as Lucy syringed a little liquid into his mouth. He seemed to like the taste and opened his dark eyes a little. Then he lapped a bit of the fish and puppy milk mixture from the spoon Lucy held out.

"That's a very good sign," said Gran. When the little otter was tired and had finished eating, Lucy helped Gran clean his sore neck. They made sure he had gone to the toilet and then popped him back snugly in his box. Gran found a hot-water bottle with a furry cover to put in the box and the little cub snuggled up next to it, closed his eyes, and went to sleep.

Chapter Three

The rest of the afternoon went very quickly—every hour they fed the little otter, and there was always so much to do looking after the birds and other animals and keeping their cages and bowls clean. Lucy put on some rubber gloves and did some washing up, and washed and disinfected the surfaces. Then she checked the shelves to see what new things Gran needed to reorder.

"We need more mealworms and milk formula, more paper towels and disposable aprons, and more gloves and bandages, Gran," she said, writing a list on the board.

"Well, Christmas is coming—maybe Father Christmas will bring them!" said Gran, sighing. "It does cost so much to keep this going." Then she smiled and gave Lucy a big hug.

"Wash your hands and then off you go home, Lucy. I'll keep an eye on everything. Thank you so much. You've been such a help today."

Lucy walked home feeling tired but happy. Her house looked very Christmassy—outside Dad had put up colored Christmas lights which twinkled on and off, and Mom had hung a Christmas

wreath on the door. Inside it was full of tinsel decorations, Christmas cards were everywhere, and the pile of Christmas presents under the tree was getting bigger every day.

Lucy didn't have much chance to tell her family about the otter at first because her brother Oscar's team had won a soccer match, and he had to tell everybody every detail of every goal over dinner. Lucy kept trying to interrupt but Oscar was too interested in his story to notice—he kept waving his arms and moving the snowmen salt and pepper shakers around the table to show who moved where and when.

"That's great, Oscar, well done," said Lucy's dad eventually. "I think maybe we should ask Lucy about her day now."

"Rosie and Sita and I rescued a baby otter today," said Lucy.

"Where did you find it?" said Oscar. "They are normally very hard to find. Are you sure it wasn't a stoat or a weasel?"

Oscar's so annoying sometimes, thought Lucy. *Just because he goes to middle school he thinks he knows everything.*

"Yes, I am sure!" replied Lucy. "Gran thinks it must have been swept out of its holt by flood waters, and then it got tangled up in some plastic trash in the river behind Rosie's house. Its neck is really sore."

"That's awful," said Oscar. "People shouldn't throw trash in the river—it's really dangerous for wildlife." Lucy stopped feeling so cross. Oscar could be a bit bossy, and his soccer stories were too long, but he was kind. Lucy could see that Merry, her cat, had crept under the table and was sitting on Oscar's feet, and he was letting her.

"How were Rosie and Sita?" said Mom.

"They're fine, but Rosie's very worried about singing in the concert at the old people's home on Christmas Eve. She's doing a solo," said Lucy.

"I'm sure she'll be wonderful," said Dad. "I've heard her sing and I'd pay to hear her! Tell her not to worry."

After dinner Lucy felt so tired she went to bed early. She got her snow globe out of her coat pocket and brought it back upstairs and put it next to her bed. Merry followed her up to her room as usual. Sometimes Merry went out at night, but she always started the night on Lucy's bed, and she was always there when Lucy woke in the morning.

Lucy brushed her teeth and put on her pajamas. Then she got into bed next to Scruffy, her pajama-case dog, and Merry. She shook the globe again and they watched the snow fall over the little Christmas scene of a cottage in a snowy wood. She felt very sleepy.

"Thank you so much, snow globe, for sending the vet to the otter," said Lucy. "Gran and I will look after him and feed him and keep him warm until he is better."

She was sure the snow globe felt warm in her hands and glowed brightly for a moment, but her eyes felt so tired they kept closing.

"Did you see that?" she said to Merry, Scruffy, and her rocking horse, Rocky, as she put the snow globe on her bedside table. Merry pushed her head against

Lucy's arm and purred, but Lucy wasn't sure if she was just trying to get her to lie down so Merry could tuck in comfortably behind her. Lucy yawned.

"Goodnight, you three. I hope the little otter and Rosie sleep well tonight," she said. It was nice to see the snow globe back on the bedside table at Christmas, and she was certain it had sent the vet to the otter. Lucy yawned and lay down and fell fast asleep, Merry snuggled up behind her, the snow in the snow globe still falling over the trees and the little house, even though Lucy had stopped shaking it a long time before.

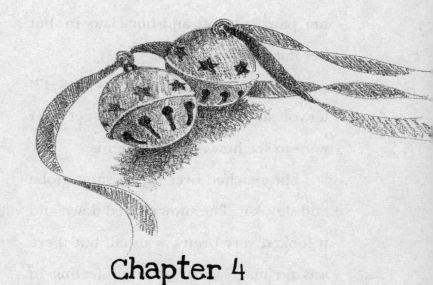

Chapter 4

"Hello Merry!" said Lucy, early the next morning. The little cat looked very sweet and comfortable stretched out on her back on Lucy's bed. Lucy stroked her soft furry tummy but Merry quickly curled on her side, keeping her eyes tightly shut, her paws still soft and her claws in, but her tail twitching a little.

"Sleepyhead!" laughed Lucy. "OK, I'll let you sleep—but I'm going to get up. I want to see how the little otter is."

She reached over to the snow globe and shook it. The snow drifted down and it looked very pretty as usual, but there was no magic glow or tingly feeling in her hands.

Lucy pulled on her cozy robe and ran downstairs for breakfast. She loved the Christmas holidays.

"Can I go and help Gran with the otter cub, Mom?" she asked, as she spread butter on her toast.

"Of course!" laughed Mom. "Be back for lunch at one, though. Sita and her mom and dad are coming over."

After breakfast Lucy put on her Wildlife Rescue Center uniform, grabbed her coat, and rushed over to Gran's. She went through the garden gate, straight through to the Center, where she found Gran already cleaning out the cages.

"Hello, Lucy!" said Gran. "You're just in time to help me feed the otter." Gran and Lucy washed their hands and put on disposable gloves.

"He's much perkier now," said Gran as they pulled the cardboard box out of the heated cage. The little otter put his short webbed feet over the side and looked at them with interest.

"I love his little whiskers!" said Lucy. "And his tiny ears! He looks so solemn!"

"Let's find out how much he weighs," said Gran, putting the little otter on the scales. The tiny creature wasn't quite sure what to do but luckily he stayed still long enough, his paws spread wide, for Gran to read his weight; then Lucy caught him just as he tried to scramble off, his long tail swishing.

Lucy was used to holding small animals, and, although the otter was very wriggly, she held him close while Gran got the feed ready. Then Lucy fed the little otter some mashed-up salmon and puppy milk formula from the spoon. He was very hungry and closed his eyes, concentrating on every mouthful. Gran had to hold him very firmly as his little paws kept reaching up to get the spoon and nearly knocked it out of Lucy's hands. His long tail moved from side to side in excitement.

"We'll clean his neck up again, but it is looking so much better already," said Gran. "I'll put him in this little playpen so he can have a run around in safety— and he can sleep in the cat basket. Can you put a soft towel in it?"

Gran refilled the hot-water bottle

and put it in the cat basket. "I have a little soft teddy he can cuddle up with, but he really needs to be with other otters as soon as possible, poor little thing!" she said. "But first I'll hold him over the cat litter tray. Do you remember what I told you otter poo was called, Lucy?"

"Spraint," said Lucy.

"Yes. They use it to mark their territory too. It might be interesting to go back down along the river this afternoon and see if we can see any spraint or paw prints in the mud," said Gran. "I wonder how far this little fellow was washed down river? It is so good you found him, Lucy, and that you got that plastic off his neck in time."

"I hate trash," said Lucy. "I remember that poor hedgehog we found with his head stuck in a plastic bag—he would have died if we hadn't found him. I don't know why people don't throw their trash away."

"It isn't just trash, either," said Gran, putting the little otter down in the playpen next to a ball. "Otters get very ill from a disease they catch from cats—but they don't get it from meeting cats. They get it when people flush cat litter down the toilet instead of putting it in the garbage can. The disease gets into the water system and rivers, and otters are very sensitive to it and can even die."

"That's awful!" said Lucy. "I didn't know that. I'm going to tell everyone at school that cat litter should be put in the garbage can, not down the toilet."

"That would be wonderful, Lucy!" said Gran. "If people just stopped doing that and were more careful about their trash that would help otters a lot."

The little otter rolled on top of the ball and pushed it around a little with his paws. Gran put down a long cardboard tube and he squeezed himself in and out, chittering excitedly.

"He's so lovely," said Lucy. "Should we put him in a bath so he can swim about?"

Gran laughed. "Lucy, as he hasn't yet learned to swim, he would HATE it! When I worked in the otter sanctuary with my friend Tom, I remember the amount of noise there was when we first put rescued baby otters in water. They squeaked so long and loudly! It's hard to believe but in the wild the otter moms have to be quite firm with their cubs. No, I think we'll leave that job to the otter sanctuary. I do hope Tom returns my call soon. This cub really needs to be with other otters and it would be too easy to fall in love with him here. Look."

The excited little otter had fallen asleep on the floor of the pen. Lucy climbed over and picked him up carefully and put him in the cat basket next to his teddy and cozy hot-water bottle.

"He'll be fine for another few hours," said Gran. "All the birds and animals are settled for now. I think I'll have some lunch and put my feet up for a bit. It's such a lovely winter's day maybe I'll go out for a walk later."

"Or a paddle?" said Lucy. "Gran, I was thinking—maybe if some of us went to the river near Rosie's we could pull out the trash that is in the reeds and stop another little river animal or bird from getting hurt. Sita and her mom and dad are coming for lunch—maybe they could help."

"That's a good idea, Lucy! Our Christmas present to the river!" said Gran. "Give me a call when you go down there and I'll get my long wader boots and join you. It shouldn't take too long if there is a team of us."

Lucy ran home and got there just in time to change out of her uniform and into her favorite reindeer sweater, wash her hands, and join Sita and her parents at lunch. Oscar's friends, Will and Fergus, were round and Dad and Mom said they could stay for pizza too, so the kitchen was very crowded. Mom said the children could take their lunch into the living room and watch television.

"I wish there was some soccer on," complained Oscar. "I don't feel like watching a Christmas film or anything like that."

There was a cartoon about a little kitten and a program about someone

building their own house, but Oscar
flicked through the channels.

"Hey! Wait!" said Fergus. "That's an
otter!"

It was a program about a family
who lived near a river, and they were

watching a group of otters swim together. The family could only see their heads as they looked above the water, and the bubbles on the surface as they dived underneath the surface of the river. The program said how mysterious and shy wild otters are and how hard they are to spot. Luckily there were underwater cameras in the river itself, and so the program showed how the otters chased fish in the river, and how they all twisted and turned and rolled together under the water. Baby otters didn't like learning to swim, but by the time they were adults they were experts.

"It's so beautiful!" said Sita.

"They have so much fun together," said Lucy, feeling sad to think of the little otter all on his own. She wondered if she could ask the snow globe for another wish.

"I love otters," said Fergus. "I used to have a great book called *Tarka the Otter*."

"So did I!" said Oscar. "And Gran adopted an otter for me for one year when I was five."

"I didn't know that!" said Lucy. "That's a lovely present! I'd like that!"

"Yes—I remember it lived at the otter sanctuary she used to work at and I used to get letters and photographs from it."

"I didn't know otters could write!"

said Will, and Oscar threw a pillow at him, narrowly missing the Christmas tree.

"Mind my pizza!" said Will.

"We rescued an otter cub yesterday," said Lucy. "It was tangled up in trash in the river, so Gran and I are going to clear out trash this afternoon so that no more otters or birds get hurt. I was going to ask if people would come and help. If lots of us go it shouldn't take long at all."

"I'll help," said Sita.

"So will I," said Fergus. "Me too," said Will, "as long as there's time to play soccer afterward."

"Who said anything about soccer?" said Sita's dad, standing at the door. "Did you hear that, Sita?"

"Can we help Lucy's gran clear out the river near Rosie's house?" said Sita. "It will only be for an hour or so."

"That's a good idea," said Sita's mom. "It's such a lovely day it will be good to get some fresh air."

"I'll see if I have any spare boots for anyone to borrow," said Mom.

"And I think I have some fishing pants I can lend too," said Dad. "We don't want anyone going for a bath!"

"I'll call Rosie," said Lucy. "I'll tell her how the little otter is and about operation Christmas clean-up! It's going to be fun!"

Chapter Five

Rosie opened the door and led Lucy and the gang through to the kitchen. Gran was already there chatting to Rosie's mom. Leah was standing up with a Christmas apron on, helping her mom stir some cake mixture, but as soon as she saw everyone she wanted to join them. She especially liked the funny Christmas hat Lucy's dad was wearing, even though Lucy and Oscar had begged him not to wear it outside the house.

"Lucy Daddy funny hat!" she cried. And "Me go too!", dropping her spoon in the bowl.

"But Leah—we're making chocolate cake now. You like making cakes," said her mom. "We'll make it into a log and decorate it."

"Me no cake. STOPPIT!" said Leah firmly, trying to pull her apron off.

"Oh dear," sighed Rosie's mom. "I suppose I'll finish quicker if Leah is with you—but you will keep an eye on her, won't you, Rosie? Keep her away from the water. You can use her safety reins— she likes them at the moment if she can pretend she is a horse or a dog."

"She can be a special reindeer if she likes," said Lucy. "Would you like that, Leah?" Leah nodded and carefully got off the chair. Sita helped her take off her apron and Rosie brought her yellow duck boots for her to put on and her red duffel coat and white hat and scarf and gloves.

"Now, Leah," said Lucy, holding her hand—she loved how small it was—"you can be a very good little reindeer called

Starlight. Reindeer don't go in rivers do they? Reindeer are very good and stay out of the water." Leah nodded her head very seriously.

"And Starlight the reindeer has reins," said Rosie, slipping them over Leah's head.

They all went down the garden and through the gate and onto the path by the river.

"We'll need to be careful as the water is a bit higher than normal, but it's still not too deep. If the adults stand in the deepest part and we all have waterproofs

on then I think we can work together in the same spot," said Gran. "I've brought some gloves if people need them, and some litter pickers. You just squeeze the handles and the jaws at the end will grab the trash. Now, if you give me Leah's reins, Leah can help me hold the bag and everyone can pass me the trash. That's a very important job to do, isn't it, Leah? We're picking up all the nasty trash that hurts animals."

At first Leah was very good as they passed the trash down, and because they were all working together they cleared a lot. The river itself wasn't too dirty, but in the reeds and plants at the side there were chip bags, candy wrappers, soda cans, and plastic bags.

Leah started fidgeting after a while so Rosie and Lucy came out of the water to help hold the bag and keep her happy.

"Let's sing some songs!" said Mom. "I know—'Jingle Bells'!" So they all sang "Jingle Bells" and then "Twinkle, Twinkle, Little Star."

"What a lovely voice you have, Rosie," said Gran.

"Yes, it's gorgeous," said Lucy's dad, smiling and looking very cheerful in his red Christmas hat.

"We keep telling her that, don't we Leah?" said Peter.

"Thank you!" said Rosie. She turned a bit red but looked very pleased.

"How are you feeling now about singing on Christmas Eve?" said Lucy quietly as the others got on with passing the trash.

"I was worrying about it all yesterday evening," said Rosie. "I know you say I'm good, but I'm still scared about singing in a concert. I'm sure I'm going to forget the words or sing a wrong note. I can't wait for it to be over."

Lucy felt really sorry for Rosie and wished her friend felt more confident.

Then Leah wanted the reindeer song, but instead of singing "Rudolf the Red-nosed Reindeer" she wanted to sing "Starlight the Red-nosed Reindeer." Leah was doing a funny little dance when Will, who was in the river wearing waders, looked down at his feet and shouted, "Hey, I can see fish!"

"Me see fish!" shouted Leah, and she ran toward the river. Luckily Lucy grabbed her reins so she didn't fall in, but she sat down with a bump on the bank, her pants got very wet, and her boots filled with water. She started to cry as Peter poured the water out of her boots onto the grass and she looked very sadly at her wet socks.

"Naughty river. Naughty water. COLD!" she said.

"Oh dear," said Peter. "I think this little reindeer has got a little bit tired. I'll take her back to the house."

Everybody waved Leah off as Peter carried her back up the garden path.

"I think this stretch of river is pretty clear now," said Gran. "Good job, everyone! I'm very pleased to see fish in it—that shows it isn't too polluted."

"I think we'd better not go back to the house just yet so that Peter can settle Leah down," said Mom.

"How about a quick soccer match

and then meet back at Rosie's?" said Dad.
"Anyone up for it if I run home and grab
a ball?"

"I am!" said Sita.

"I think I'd like to walk along the
river a little way and see if I can see any
signs of otters," said Gran.

"Can I come?" said Rosie. "I'm not as
keen on soccer as Sita."

"Nobody could be as keen on soccer
as Sita—except Oscar!" laughed Lucy.

As Lucy, Rosie, and Gran walked
away from the backs of the houses, the
river became quieter and more peaceful.
They stopped talking and listened to the
sounds of the river and the trees beside

it—the rustling of birds in hedges, the water as it flowed over some rocks, a duck quacking somewhere.

"Look!" Gran said. "Did you see that!"

They had all seen a flash of blue.

"That was a kingfisher, girls!" said Gran. "What a wonderful sight! I love those river birds so much!"

Lucy looked down on the ground.

"Gran—look! I think I see some footprints in the mud by the water's edge!"

"Clever girl! Those are otter prints. And look—some otter spraint. You can see that it has eaten some fish—look at the fish bones. So this is a message to any other otters that this is an otter's territory."

"I wonder if it is our otter's mom or dad?" said Lucy.

"We can't know, as our cub may have been washed down quite a distance because of the flooding. But at least this river has otters in it—that's a good thing," said Gran.

"Shall we go home and have some hot chocolate?" said Rosie. "I'm getting a bit cold now."

"Me too," said Lucy.

"I think I'll go home and feed that little otter and give Tom another call," said Gran. "I really want that otter back in the wild as soon as possible. The longer he is away from it and other otters, the harder it will be to get him back there. I'll take this shortcut home now—you go back to Rosie's house, Lucy. Thanks for all your help."

"I'll come and see you later," promised Lucy.

It was getting dark by the time Lucy and Rosie got back to the house. They could see the Christmas tree twinkling inside. It looked so welcoming.

When they got through the door

everyone was inside happily talking about the soccer match. Mom had saved a goal, and Oscar and Sita had both scored one, so they were very pleased. Lucy's dad was complaining because he said Lucy's mom had stopped his goal, and Sita's parents were laughing at him. Oscar, Will, and Fergus were enjoying the cake Rosie's mom had made. Leah came downstairs smiling after her nap and got in a terrible mess eating her piece of "choclit log," as she called it. It was delicious, and with hot chocolate was the perfect thing to have after working on the river.

"What a lovely Christmas vacation we are having!" said Rosie's mom, looking round at everyone.

"Mom only thinks that because she doesn't have to sing in front of everyone," whispered Rosie to Lucy, looking miserable again. "It's spoiling my Christmas."

Chapter Six

Lucy went back home as soon as she left Rosie's, changed into her uniform, and went straight over to Gran's. She carefully picked up the little otter out of his playpen. He didn't seem at all frightened now. His fur was so soft and his whiskers tickled her as he wriggled up onto her shoulder, but she caught him and held him firmly so that Gran could check his neck.

"He ate a lot just before you came and his neck is looking so much better!" said Gran. As if to prove it the otter gave a big wriggle and jumped off Lucy's lap, running straight to her boots and climbing into one. It tipped over with his weight and he squeaked and poked his head out.

"Naughty!" laughed Lucy. Gran picked up the boot and soon the otter was back in his pen.

"He's just a baby," said Gran, "but I

really don't want him to get too used to us."

"He's so sweet and soft and roly-poly," said Lucy. "I do wish I could take him home."

"Oh dear—don't wish for that, Lucy," said Gran. "If you are going to wish for anything, wish for him to get a place at the sanctuary. I'm afraid we are both getting too fond of him. One day we'll go together and see some grown wild otters—it's much more magical than having one as a pet."

Lucy wasn't sure. As she walked home she thought about her magic snow globe. Lucy wondered if it would be wrong to wish on the snow globe to keep the wild otter cub, but she knew deep down it would be and that Gran was right. She felt sad. "I'll miss him so much," she said to herself. Luckily, when she got home her own pet, Merry the cat, spent most of the evening purring, curled up on Lucy's lap, which made her feel much better.

Lucy got into bed and looked at the snow globe. She remembered what Gran had said: "If you wish for anything, wish for him to get a place at the sanctuary." She could wish on the snow globe for the otter and she could wish on the snow globe for Rosie.

"But if I wish for a place at the sanctuary for him I won't see my little otter again," Lucy said out loud. "Anyway, the magic snow globe sent the vet. That probably used all the magic up. I'm sure there aren't any wishes left."

And she turned her back on the snow globe so she couldn't see its gentle glow, and fell asleep. But in her dreams the little otter was very sad, and then she had a dream that Rosie was crying because of having to sing her solo at the concert. Lucy was glad to get up in the morning. Looking at the snow globe made her feel funny inside.

"I don't think there is room for the snow globe on my table," said Lucy to Rocky, Merry, and Scruffy. "I have to wrap lots of presents and I need somewhere to put the tape and the scissors. I don't want to knock it on the floor and break it. I'll put it in the closet so it is safe."

She didn't look at Scruffy, Merry, or Rocky when she put the snow globe away. She didn't think they'd understand or agree with her.

"I'm sure there is no magic left in it anyway," she said out loud, as she closed the closet door.

But she wasn't really.

The next couple of days were very busy.

Merry got in the way as Lucy wrapped presents and wrote cards. Lucy, Sita, and Rosie went Christmas shopping and Lucy bought a beautiful scarf for Mom, some Christmas socks for Dad, a book about soccer for Oscar, and a book about an animal sanctuary for Gran.

"I can't wait for Gran to open this!" she said to Merry when she brought it home and wrapped it up. Merry patted the tape and Lucy remembered how Merry used to play with it when she was a kitten.

"You're still a naughty little cat!" Lucy laughed, and Merry purred and rubbed herself up against her as if she agreed.

Lucy and Sita went back to Rosie's and played with Leah. They told her stories and played skittles bowl and a game where you had to throw hoops over some toys. Leah thought it was wonderful and they played it so often Lucy got quite good at it. Then

Rosie and Lucy went over to Sita's to make meat pies, but it wasn't as much fun as it normally was. Rosie looked tired and worried, and Lucy wondered if it was because of the singing. But somehow, Lucy couldn't think of the words to make Rosie feel better, and Rosie didn't really want to talk about it with her.

Every day, Lucy popped over to Gran's Wildlife Rescue Center to see the baby otter. Oscar came too on the day before Christmas Eve.

"As soon as Gran finds a place at the sanctuary, the otter really does have to go," Oscar said when they were walking home after the visit.

"Why does everyone keep saying that?" said Lucy crossly, and stomped off. She hardly spoke to anyone all evening, and she went to bed feeling miserable. The magic snow globe was still in the closet, and she missed its gentle glow. She didn't feel very Christmassy without it, but if she took it out she would have to think about wishes. And she really didn't want to.

And then all of a sudden it was Christmas Eve.

"I'll go and check on the otter before the concert, shall I, Gran?" said Lucy to

Gran, who had come over for lunch. "I won't be long."

"That would be kind of you," said Gran. "Could you check the other animals have enough water too?"

It was nice to be out walking in the quiet, fresh air. It made Lucy happy to think of Father Christmas and his reindeer moving across the world to deliver presents. Lucy thought of all the animals she had helped since she had become Gran's special assistant. Lucy remembered the first baby rabbit and she was glad he was back, snug and cozy with his family. At least she had a lovely rabbit badge on her sweatshirt to remind her of him. She loved wearing the uniform Gran had made her whenever she went to the Center. It was so special to be Gran's wildlife rescue assistant.

At the Center, Lucy let the little otter out of his cage and he ran around the pen. He had made a little mess in the cat litter tray, so Lucy carefully lifted it out and emptied it into the garbage can.

Then she washed her hands and went back to the pen.

But the little otter was gone. Lucy must have nudged the sides of the pen a little when she stepped out, and he must have squeezed himself out the side.

"Oh no!" said Lucy.

Luckily she could hear his excited chittering, and she saw him by the door. But then he turned and she saw his tail disappear through the cat flap. He was out in the dark garden, where there was a pond and all sorts of dangers for a baby otter who hadn't learned to swim.

"What can I do?" said Lucy, grabbing some thick gloves. She looked around

and saw some towels folded in the bottom of a laundry basket. Lucy grabbed a towel to throw over the otter—but then she had an even better idea. She put the rest of the towels on the side, grabbed the empty basket, and ran out.

"Please may he not have gone far," she said under her breath, looking all around the garden. "Please may he not get hurt."

Chapter Seven

The next few minutes felt like hours for
Lucy. She looked around the sheds and
down the path, but could see nothing.
She ran to the pond, because that would
be a dangerous place for him, but he
wasn't there. Then she spotted him, on

the lawn by a garden gnome.

"Magic snow globe, I know you're not here, but please help me!" Lucy said, and threw the basket. As the basket flew through the air Lucy was sure she saw a flash of something like a stream of glittering stars, and heard a gentle tinkling of bells.

The basket landed on the otter and the garden gnome. The otter was trapped! It gave lots of indignant whistles and squeaks, and the basket started to shuffle as the otter tried to get out. The good thing was that, although the basket moved a little, the garden gnome inside made it too heavy for the little otter to

get far. Lucy felt so relieved she wanted to laugh, but she knew there wasn't time— she didn't want him to wriggle out again.

"Lucy—what's happening?" came Gran's voice from the doorway. "You took such a long time to come home I thought I'd come and check on you."

"Bring the cat basket, Gran," called Lucy. "It's all right—the otter escaped but I've got him under the laundry basket."

Gran rushed out and together, using the towel, they grabbed the very cross otter cub and got him back in the cat basket.

"Thank you!" said Lucy to the garden gnome as she put him straight and back in his place on the lawn.

The otter was furious that his adventure had stopped, and, when they brought him in and put him back in his cage, he made a lot of noise to tell them so.

"I'm so sorry, Gran," said Lucy, over the indignant cries. "He must have squeezed out the side of the pen when I was emptying the litter tray. Then he ran out through the cat flap."

"All's well that ends well," said Gran. "You did a wonderful job catching him. But I think this really proves he needs to be somewhere else. It's just a shame it will have to wait until after Christmas now. Oh well, we've tried our best."

I haven't, thought Lucy. *I haven't tried my best for the otter and I haven't tried my best for Rosie. I knew deep down I could have wished on the snow globe for them both, but I put it away instead so I wouldn't have to think about it and I could pretend the magic had run out.*

Lucy rushed back home and got the snow globe out of the closet. She held it in her hands and sat on the bed with Scruffy and a sleepy Merry.

"Magic snow globe—thank you for helping me catch the little otter. I know he needs to grow up with other otters and go back to the river when he is ready. Please may it not be too late to wish for a place in the sanctuary for the little otter in time for Christmas. I should have wished for that before but I didn't want you to grant my wish. I wanted to keep the little otter forever, but I know that won't make him happy. Oh, and one last thing: please can you also help my friend Rosie—please can you give her the confidence to sing her solo at the concert later."

The snow globe glowed gently and Rocky gave a gentle rock. Merry purred and she was sure Scruffy's little pajama-case tail gave a little wag.

Lucy shook the snow globe. "I wish that the little otter will be with other otters this Christmas, and I wish that Rosie won't feel nervous tonight."

The snow fell faster and faster on the woodland scene, turning white and silver and red, orange, yellow, green, blue, indigo, and violet. Then the wood disappeared and suddenly there were lots of sparkling patterns in the globe—lots of tiny glittering musical notes and then lots of tiny little otter shapes swimming and turning and rolling together. It was so pretty to watch. The globe felt warm and comforting in her hands, and Lucy felt a tingling fizzy happiness creep from her toes, up to her head, and along her arms. She could imagine just how happy

and free an otter felt swimming in the river.

Then the snow turned white again, and the little house and the woods were back.

"I know what I have to do now," said Lucy, and she ran downstairs to call Rosie.

When Rosie answered she sounded very quiet and sad.

"Rosie," said Lucy. "I just want to tell you not to be scared. We will all be there to support you at the concert."

"I know," said Rosie. "But what if it goes wrong?"

"It won't," said Lucy. "Remember we have all heard you singing before.

Remember when we cleared the river and everyone said how lovely your voice was. I know you will be great. Just imagine you are singing for Leah—close your eyes and pretend you are singing to her in bed like you always do. Everything will be fine."

"Are you sure?" said Rosie.

"Completely," said Lucy.

"Thank you, Lucy—you're such a great friend," said Rosie. "I do feel so much better already."

When Lucy put down the phone she felt so much better too. It suddenly felt like it was truly Christmas at last.

Lucy, Oscar, Gran, and Mom and Dad joined Peter and Nina and Leah and Sita and her family in the residents' lounge to hear the choir sing.

Leah was sitting on her grandad's knee, but she was getting a bit wriggly and loud.

"Do you girls want to come with me and feed the little birdies," Grandad said, taking Leah's hand. Leah looked very pleased—she loved her grandad and loved him to tell stories about his farm. He was very old now and walked with a cane, but he still had very twinkly eyes, and always looked after the birds in the garden.

They went outside and checked that there were plenty of fat balls and seeds in the bird feeder. A little blue tit flew away into the dusk as they arrived.

"Look!" Grandad said suddenly, pointing his cane toward the bottom of the garden.

"Doggy!" shouted Leah excitedly.

"What was it?" said Lucy.

"An otter!" smiled Grandad. "The garden goes down to the river, and some of the fish have been taken from the pond. I thought there might be otters about!"

"So the doggy Leah kept saying she saw was an otter!" said Sita.

"Clever girl!" said Lucy.

"Look!" pointed Leah. "Reindeer!"

They looked up in the darkening sky and saw a little flashing light moving. Lucy had told Leah a story about Father Christmas's littlest reindeer guiding the sleigh as he flew to deliver presents.

"Starlight!" said Leah proudly, and Lucy gave her a hug.

"That's right!" said Lucy. "Starlight the reindeer is in the sky helping Father Christmas because it's Christmas Eve!"

"The concert's starting!" called Lucy's mom from the patio doors, and they went back inside. Lucy saw Rosie standing at the front of the choir and remembered her wish on the snow globe again.

"Please may Rosie not be nervous," Lucy said under her breath.

Just in time Rosie's dad arrived. He waved at Rosie and sat down in the front row.

Then Rosie closed her eyes and began to sing.

Chapter Eight

Rosie's voice sounded wonderful. Even Leah was quiet. She sat, snuggled up on her grandad's lap, and sucked her thumb as Rosie sang the first verse of a beautiful Christmas carol. When Rosie had finished her verse she opened her eyes and smiled, and the choir and the people sitting in the lounge joined in the rest of the verses. Lucy saw Rosie's grandad wipe a happy tear from his eye as everyone applauded the choir at the end. Everyone agreed that Rosie's solo had been the best they had ever heard. Rosie's dad gave her a big hug and Lucy could see how happy that made Rosie. It was special that he had come to hear her too. Peter and her mom came over and they were all smiling and talking together.

"That was marvelous, Rosie love," Rosie's grandad said, when Rosie gave him a kiss.

"It was wonderful," said Sita.

"You sounded amazing!" said Lucy.

"Thank you!" said Rosie, beaming. "And it was a miracle, because I wasn't nervous at all. I just remembered what you told me Lucy, I imagined I was singing to Leah, and I felt confident. Thank you so much."

"Thank you snow globe," whispered Lucy under her breath.

"Look—there are homemade meat pies!" said Sita's mom. Oscar and the girls passed them around to everyone, and they drank tea and opened party favors. Everyone put on Christmas hats and read jokes from their party favors. Leah insisted on doing a dance in the middle of the lounge, and was very pleased when everyone clapped. She got a bit overexcited and didn't want to stop, but luckily Grandad had a present to give her, and she was very pleased when she ripped

the paper off and found it was a toy lamb.

"Like the little lambs I had on my farm and kept warm in my kitchen," smiled Grandad, and gave Leah a kiss.

That reminded Lucy of the otter being warmed up.

The manager of the home gave out Christmas bingo cards. There were lots of pictures of Christmassy things—desserts, donkeys, stars, party favors, and presents—and people had to match them to the cards she would pull out of a hat. It was lots of fun. Then Gran's cell phone rang.

"That's funny—I thought I'd switched it off," she said as she took it out of her bag. "I'm so glad it didn't ring during the concert."

"Hello? Really? How wonderful! Tonight? That is the best Christmas present you could give me! Thanks, Tom! See your brother in ten minutes then! Bye!"

Gran finished the call with a big smile on her face.

"That was my good friend, Tom, from the otter sanctuary. He says they have a place for the otter! His brother is driving down to visit him for Christmas, and they have realized he will be passing through here in the next half an hour and he can pick up the otter cub on the way. Isn't that wonderful? Our baby otter will be with other otters for Christmas! Do you want to come with me, Lucy, and get him ready for his new home?"

Lucy ran and gave Rosie and Sita a hug and rushed off with Gran.

The otter loudly complained in the warm cat basket Gran got ready for him, even though he had his teddy and hot-water bottle. Lucy smiled at Gran.

"I just hope that he stops making all that noise or Tom's brother will have an awful car journey with him."

"I think I need a nice cup of tea," said Gran. "And I think you deserve one of your presents a little early."

Gran passed Lucy a little package. Lucy smiled when she opened it and saw what was inside. It was a tiny model of an otter and a new badge for her uniform with an otter on it.

"Thanks, Gran," Lucy said, and gave Gran a big hug. "I definitely won't forget how I got this badge!"

Lucy noticed that the otter had gone quiet. *He must have tired himself out with all his complaining*, she thought. Lucy peered inside the cat basket and saw him curled up next to his teddy, asleep.

"When you wake up you will get a lovely surprise!" she whispered to him. "You're very sweet now but you definitely need to be with other otters. You're going to learn to swim and then go back to the wild. You will have a lovely time! Merry Christmas!"

Tom's brother arrived and was very nice. He stayed and had a cup of tea with them and Lucy told him all about rescuing the otter and how they had cleared trash out of the river so another animal wouldn't get hurt.

Then he took the little otter in his cat basket and drove off.

Lucy waved him off. "Goodbye little otter," she whispered.

"See you tomorrow, Lucy," said Gran, "and thank you for being such a wonderful assistant and lovely granddaughter. I love you very much."

"I love you too, Gran," said Lucy, and they gave each other a big hug.

When Lucy got home she called Sita and Rosie to explain what had happened before the concert. They both laughed when she told them about throwing the basket over the otter and they arranged to meet up after Christmas.

Lucy was getting ready for bed when Gran called with exciting news.

"Tom just called," said Gran. "He was so impressed to hear about you clearing the river that he has invited us all down to the sanctuary after Christmas. He is going to give us a special V.I.P. tour and we can see our baby otter and meet the otters he is going to live with."

"That's so wonderful!" said Lucy. "I

can't wait to see him in the sanctuary. He is going to have such a lot of fun!"

Lucy took her little otter model and put it next to the snow globe by her bed.

"Thank you for hearing my wish in the garden when the otter escaped," said Lucy to the snow globe. "And thank you for working magic again and helping the otter get well. I'm so glad he is going to be safe in the sanctuary and go back to the wild. And thank you for helping Rosie feel confident."

Then she put on her pajamas, brushed her teeth, checked that her Christmas stocking was hung up at the end of her bed, and, patting Rocky, got into bed. She put her arms around Merry and Scruffy and went straight to sleep.

It was Christmas morning.

Lucy sat up and looked in her stocking. It was full of lovely things. There was a book called *Tarka the Otter*, some chocolate coins in a little purse with a picture of a baby reindeer on it, and a notebook with a picture of a baby rabbit on it. There was a calendar with otters on it too.

"I can write the date on it that we are going to visit the otter sanctuary!" said

Lucy happily.

There was even a small cat toy for Merry and two ribbons—so Lucy put one on Scruffy and the other she tied around Rocky's neck.

Then Lucy noticed that the magic snow globe was glowing softly and there was a folded piece of paper sticking out from under it. As she pulled it out and opened it there was the sound of sleigh bells and the paper sparkled. The letter was written in lovely big curly writing, and reading it made her feel very, very happy.

Well done Lucy!

The Christmas magic came from you this year. Well done for being such a good kind friend, for making the river safe for the birds and animals, and for saving a very special little otter.

xxx

Then Lucy looked over at the snow globe, and she saw that it was lightly snowing inside, even though she had not shaken it. In the woods she could see a little figure dressed in red with a long white beard who was waving at her. Beside him in front of the cottage was a sweet little reindeer, whose white fur sparkled, and who gave a little jump as if to say "hello."

Merry jumped on Lucy's knee and purred loudly, rubbing her head against Lucy's chin. Her fur was so soft and Lucy felt so happy inside that everything was fine.

Lucy looked at the otter model Gran

had given her and felt excited to think of what a wonderful Christmas the little cub would have with the other otters. "See you soon, my little otter," Lucy said, and as the snow in the snow globe stopped falling magically by itself, and the little figure in red and the tiny white reindeer disappeared from view, Lucy went downstairs to join her family and begin another wonderful Christmas Day.

Thank you . . .

I have had a lovely time researching otters for this book: watching sweet videos of baby otters on YouTube or wonderful documentaries which have otters in them, like *Halcyon River Diaries*, and reminding myself of books like *Tarka the Otter* by Henry Williamson or *Ring of Bright Water* by Gavin Maxwell. I also read a very good book about otters called *Otter Country: In Search of the Wild Otter* by Miriam Darlington.

I am also very lucky because I don't live very far away from the Wildwood Trust. I want to say a special thank you to Wildwood's Head of Education, Angus Carpenter, who passed on very helpful suggestions about the sort of trouble a wild baby otter could get into and why they would need to be rescued. If you are ever near Wildwood do go and visit—there are so many animals to see and learn about there.

I also want to say an especially big thank you to Tom Cox, the otter keeper at Buckfast Butterflies & Dartmoor Otter Sanctuary. He gave me wonderful advice about looking after baby otters. I am really excited as he has invited me to visit the sanctuary one day. I can't wait! You can even sponsor an otter there, like Lucy's Gran does!

About the author

Every Christmas, Anne used to ask for a dog.
She had to wait many years, but now she has
two dogs, called Timmy and Ben. Timmy is a
big, gentle golden retriever who loves people
and food and is scared of cats. Ben is a small
brown and white cavalier King Charles spaniel
who is a bit like a cat because he curls up in the
warmest places and bosses Timmy about. He
snuffles and snorts quite a lot and you can tell
what he is feeling by the way he walks. He has
a particularly pleased patter when he has stolen
something he shouldn't have, which gives him
away immediately. Anne lives in a village in Kent
and is not afraid of spiders.

Feed the birds with a homemade bird cake!

Why don't you make this quick and easy bird cake, then you can watch the birds as they come to feed, just like Rosie's grandad!

You will need an assistant, so make sure an adult helps you

What you will need:

Clean yogurt containers

Mixing bowl

Scissors

String

Lard

Any of the following:

birdseed; grated cheese; raisins; other dried fruit (but not coconut); unsalted peanuts; oats

(the best ratio is around one part lard to two parts dry mixture—add the dry mixture gradually to make sure it all sticks together)

What to do

※ Make a small hole in the bottom of each yogurt container.

※ Thread the string through the hole and tie a knot on the inside. Leave enough string on the outside so that it can be tied to a branch or a bird feeder.

※ Let the lard warm up to room temperature, then cut it up into small pieces and put it in the mixing bowl.

※ Gradually add the rest of the ingredients into the bowl, squeezing it all together with your fingers until it's bound together.

※ Fill the yogurt containers with the mixture, and put it in the fridge for about an hour, until they're set.

※ Cut through and peel away the yogurt containers.

※ Hang the containers from a branch or bird feeder, and wait for the birds to come flocking!